D1030638

R U
Ready to see?
Ready to be?
Ready to go?
Ready to Know?
Then you must be full of CURIOSITY!

Diane Terry

Text copyright 2014 Diane Terry
Illustrations copyright 2014 Rachel K. Ackerman
All rights reserved   First Edition
Published by Oren Village, L.L.C, Battle Creek, Michigan
For information or permission to reproduce, please contact
Diane Terry @dianeterryauthor.com
Text set in Baskerville. Cover design by Libby Carruth Krock.
Illustrations rendered in pencil, acrylic paint and pastel.

PUBLISHERS'S CATALOGING IN PUBLICATION DATA

Terry, Diane.

Sweetlips / by Diane Terry ; illustrations by Rachel K. Ackerman. -- First edition.
-- Battle Creek, Michigan : Oren Village, [2014]

p. ; cm.

ISBN: 978-0-9912672-1-7

Audience: Grades K-5.

Summary: Charlie and Sophia were about to take their first dive in the Seas
of Sulawesi. Uncle Gordy promised them that here they would find treasure, but
neither of them could have ever imagined what amazing treasure they were
about to discover ... all with the help of a very special fish called Sweetlips.--
Publisher.

1. Scuba diving--Indonesia--Lembeh Strait--Juvenile fiction. 2. Tropical fish--
Indonesia--Lembeh Strait--Juvenile fiction. 3. Coral reefs and islands--Indonesia-
-Lembeh Strait--Juvenile fiction. 4. Marine biodiversity--Indonesia--Lembeh
Strait-- Juvenile fiction. 5. Nudibranchia--Indonesia--Lembeh Strait-- Juvenile
fiction. 6. Blue-ringed octopuses--Indonesia-- Lembeh Strait--Juvenile fiction.
7. Shrimps--Indonesia--Lembeh Strait-- Juvenile fiction. 8. Curiosity in children--
Juvenile fiction. 9. Treasure troves--Juvenile fiction. 10. [Scuba diving-- Indone-
sia--Lembeh Strait--Fiction. 11. Tropical fish--Indonesia-- Lembeh Strait--Fiction.
12. Coral reefs and islands--Indonesia-- Lembeh Strait--Fiction. 13. Biodiversity-
-Indonesia--Lembeh Strait--Fiction. 14. Sea slugs--Indonesia--Lembeh Strait--
Fiction. 15. Octopuses--Indonesia--Lembeh Strait--Fiction. 16. Shrimps-- Indone-
sia--Lembeh Strait--Fiction. 17. Curiosity--Fiction. 18. Buried treasure--Fiction.]
19. Adventure stories. I. Ackerman, Rachel K. II. Title. III. Title: Sweet lips.

Printed in Korea

PZ7.T279 S94 2014

[Fic]--dc23   1409

SWEETLIPS

By Diane Terry   Illustrations By Rachel K. Ackerman

Gordy,
Thanks for your expertise
on the amazing underwater
world of Sulawesi.

The breezes were gently blowing as Charlie and Sophia awoke to a beautiful day! Here they were, living on a boat with Uncle Gordy in Sulawesi; an island in Indonesia found halfway around the world. For the past year they had taken scuba diving lessons at Uncle Gordy's dive shop preparing for this special trip. It was *here* that Uncle Gordy *promised* they would find amazing treasures!

"Can you believe we're going to be treasure hunters?" whispered Charlie to Sophia as they checked their air tanks. "I've read about pirates and their stolen bounty! Just to think we might discover gold doubloons, silver coins, jewels!"

"Buried treasure here we come!" giggled Sophia.

"Good morning, gang!" said Uncle Gordy. "I am so excited to take you diving today. But first, I'd like you to meet Opo, our guide! He knows these waters very well and will be able to help us find the treasures of Sulawesi!"

"Welcome, kids! Today we shall explore the coral reefs. Keep your eyes and ears open!" said Opo with a twinkle in his eye. "I promise you won't be disappointed!"

Uncle Gordy grabbed his camera. "Is everyone ready?" he asked.

With a nod and a smile they all climbed overboard.

As they descended into the cool clear water, Opo swam toward the reef and called, "Sweetlips, where are you?"

A pretty striped fish with huge yellow lips swam toward them. "Howdy, Opo! Who have you brought to the reefs today?"

"My friends, Charlie and Sophia," said Opo.

Sophia was shocked that the fish had spoken to them!

Charlie just stared at the huge lips.

"Come! Let's explore the reefs!" said Sweetlips. "There's so much to see!"

Sweeetlips lead the way pointing out beautiful emperor angelfish and weird hairy filefish.

"What is that adorable black polka dotted fish?" asked Sophia.

"I'm a barramundi and considered a tasty delight, but please don't eat me for your dinner tonight!" begged the fish.

"Eat you? No way! You're gorgeous!" exclaimed Sophia. The barramundi smiled and darted off.

Charlie turned to Opo and asked, "What's that strange grinding noise?"

Opo laughed, "That's the parrotfish dining on coral! They bite, chew, and digest it. Then out it comes as sand making the beaches of the world."

Charlie grinned. He stopped suddenly and stared at a shaggy fish walking on its fins. It had a worm like lure dangling from its head.

"Hey, Big Mouth, you catching anything today?" shouted Sweetlips.

"Even though we frogfish can expand our mouth and stomach to twice our size, it takes at least a couple of tries to catch our prey! I'll catch something soon. Have a nice day!" said the frogfish.

Sweetlips led the group toward a giant clam four foot wide weighing about four hundred and fifty pounds. They watched with fascination as it opened and closed its mouth.

Nearby a hawksbill turtle winked hello as he nibbled on sponges.

Opo swam toward some gorgonian coral.

"Take these magnifying glasses, kids, and look closely at this coral," he said. "Pygmy seahorses are attached to it."

"I don't see anything!" said Charlie.

"Oh! There's one!" shouted Sophia. "Why it blends in perfectly! They're very tiny!"

Sweetlips moved some algae. "Check out these cool ghost pipefish hanging upside down eating through their noses," he said. "Most divers never see them because of their great camouflage."

"Incredible!" gasped Charlie.

"What's that unusual fish over there?"asked Sophia.

"Sophia, what you see-a is a rhinopia!" laughed Sweetlips.

"His face is dragging, is he hurt?" asked Charlie.

"No! He's fishing! As his prey swim up for a closer look, his bucket-mouth sucks them in like a vacuum cleaner!" chuckled Uncle Gordy.

"The creatures are amazing here on the reefs, but so are the sponges!" exclaimed Sophia. "Purple, red, green and blue. There's even pink and yellow, too!"

"Right you are," said Opo. "Look closely on the sponges! There you'll find nudibranchs, colorful sea slugs that eat the sponges."

While studying the nudibranchs, Sophia's eyes grew large with fright! She'd come eye to eye with a blue ribbon eel. She backed away slowly.

Just then Charlie noticed an enormous sea snake swimming behind him!

"Easy," said Opo softly to the children. "The banded sea snake's poison is dangerous, but he's hunting for food, not us."

The sea snake swam under Charlie's leg straight toward the eel and bit its head off, then slowly devoured it. The divers watched in silent amazement.

A short time later the group waved farewell to Sweetlips. They surfaced, boarded the ship, and chatted excitedly about all they'd learned on the day's dive.

As evening arrived, Uncle Gordy announced, "Sleep well tonight and relax tomorrow. Save your energy for our night dive."

"Night dive!" the kids shouted.

"Yes, tomorrow we'll dive with lights to see unbelievable sights," said Opo.

"Will Sweetlips be there?" asked Sophia.

Opo winked.

"Now off to bed with you!" said Uncle Gordy.

The next day the kids slept late. They ate lunch and looked at Uncle Gordy's pictures. He had some terrific shots!

At dusk, the group gathered on deck. Each diver grabbed a light before stepping overboard into the inky black water.

"This is creepy," said Sophia. "Uncle Gordy, where are you? Uncle Gordy! My light's not working!"

"I'm on your right," said Uncle Gordy calmly. "Here take my light!"
He took hers and hit it repeatedly against his air tank. Finally, it lit! Opo led
them all the way down to the murky bottom.

Soon Charlie noticed movement. "Hi, Sweetlips!" he grinned.

"Hi, gang! I'm searching the bottom for food. Be careful! On my right is a fire urchin! His beautiful spines are very poisonous. On your left is another poisonous bottom dweller, who can give electrical shocks - it's a stargazer!"

"He looks like a scary skeleton!" said Charlie. "I never knew such things existed! I wish my friends could see these!"

Time seemed to stand still as the group explored the ocean bottom.

"That's Penny, a peacock mantis shrimp," said Sweetlips. "Her eyes will drive you crazy! Each one moves by itself – up, down, and all around! She's a looker! Penny packs a powerful punch with her front claws, so stay clear!"

"Sweetlips, our dive's been very interesting," said Opo observing his watch, "but it's time for us to surface!"

The kids begged to stay longer, but Opo knew what was best.

That night, two tired kids found it difficult to sleep as they discussed their amazing discoveries.

The following afternoon, Charlie questioned Uncle Gordy, "Will we search for buried treasure today?"

"Why, Charlie, haven't you seen the treasure on our dives?" asked Uncle Gordy.

"Where?" asked Sophia. "Were jewels or coins on the reefs or buried in the sand? How did we miss them?"

"You didn't," smiled Opo. "The treasures of Sulawesi are the unique sea life you have seen and spoken with, the corals and sponges that feed them, the amazing land that is home to all of them. What coins or jewels can compare with what you have seen?"

"We've explored, discovered, and learned so much here in Sulawesi," said Uncle Gordy. "Curiosity led us here and now we get to take a sense of wonder and excitement home with us."

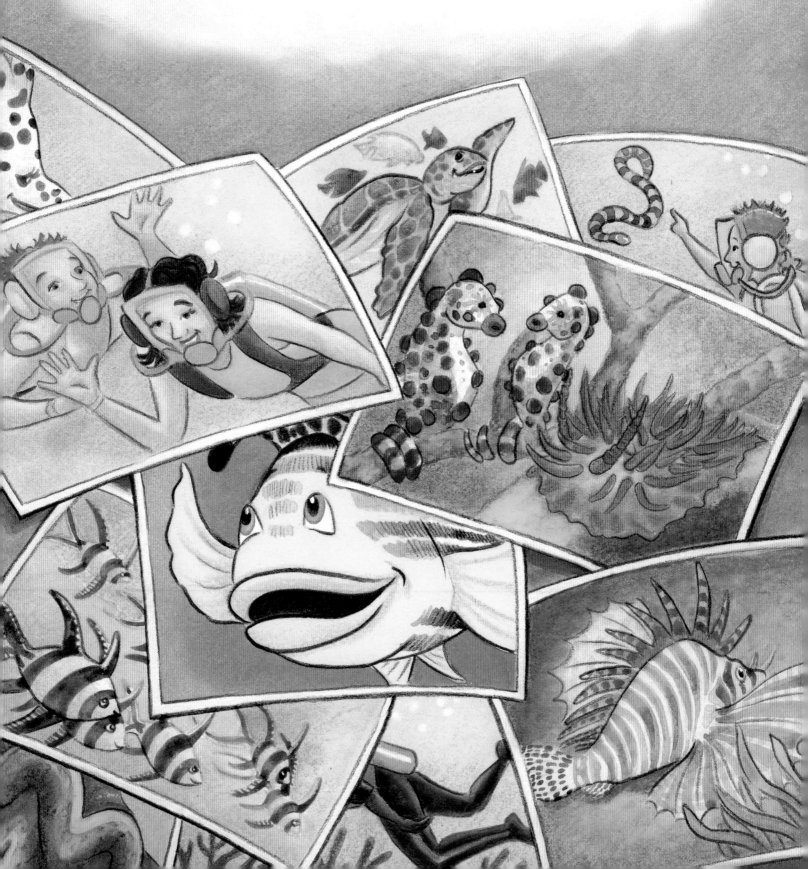

"You're right!" said Charlie. "Our dives have been unforgettable!"

"Uncle Gordy, your pictures are the best souvenirs ever," said Sophia. I can't wait to share them with our friends. Even after we do though, they won't believe these things really exist."

"I know," said Uncle Gordy. "But we know they do."

"Think we could find some treasure buried in a bun?" laughed Charlie. "I'm starving!"

Opo chuckled as the gang headed to the galley to eat. Sweetlips and today's adventure would have to wait until after lunch.